and
PETTING ZOO

# The Christmas Crocodile

# The Christmas Crocodile

by Bonny Becker

illustrated by David Small

Aladdin Paperbacks

New York London Toronto Sydney Singapore

For Doug
love, Bonny

To Sarah
love
David

First Aladdin Paperbacks edition October 2001


Aladdin Paperbacks
An imprint of Simon & Schuster
Children's Publishing Division
1230 Avenue of the Americas
New York, NY 10020



Also available in a Simon & Schuster Books for Young Readers hardcover edition.
Designed by Lucille Chomowicz
The text for this book was set in Italian Garamond.
The illustrations were rendered in watercolor and pen and black ink.
Printed in Hong Kong
10 9 8 7 6 5 4 3 2 1

The Library of Congress has cataloged the hardcover edition as follows:
Becker, Bonny.
The Christmas Crocodile / by Bonny Becker ; illustrated by David Small.
p. cm.
Summary: A very hungry crocodile is mistakenly delivered to the wrong address and
thoroughly disrupts the Christmas celebrations of Alice Jayne and her family.
ISBN 0-689-81503-4 (hc.)
[1. Crocodiles-Fiction. 2. Christmas-Fiction.] I. Small, David, ill. II. Title.
PZ7.B3814Ch 1998
[E]-dc21
96-53140
ISBN 0-689-84666-5 (Aladdin pbk.)

The Christmas Crocodile didn't mean to be bad, not really. Alice Jayne found him on Christmas Eve under the tree. He wore a red bow around his neck. It was lovely. Except he ate it.

Then he ate a couple of presents, just little ones, and he gnawed on Father's shoe, ate the wreath in the hall, and ran away with the Christmas roast—a big one. He was eating up Christmas and no one knew what to do with him.

"Send the beast to Africa," huffed Uncle Theodore, who had once hunted wild game there.

"He must be put in an orphanage," fretted Aunt Figgy, who worried a lot, especially about orphans.

“Lock him in the back room, Alice Jayne,” instructed Father, “while we consider the situation.”

“Better give him the pumpkin pie,” said Mother. “He still looks hungry.”

Alice Jayne crossed her arms and tapped her toe while the Christmas Crocodile slunk into the back room. She closed and locked the door with a firm click.

But then she thought she heard him sniffling in there. Not feeling hungry after all, she slipped him the pineapple upside-down cake, along with the pie.

"We could make him into a pair of shoes," said Uncle Theodore, who was busy considering things back in the parlor.

"Or a pet for some orphans," said Aunt Figgy.

"I wonder whose presents he ate?" said Cousin Elwood, who had finally finished eating all the fudge the Crocodile had missed and could now speak.

"He's nice," said Alice Jayne. "Maybe we could keep him."

"Unheard of!" protested Aunt Figgy.

"But it's Christmas!" said Alice Jayne.

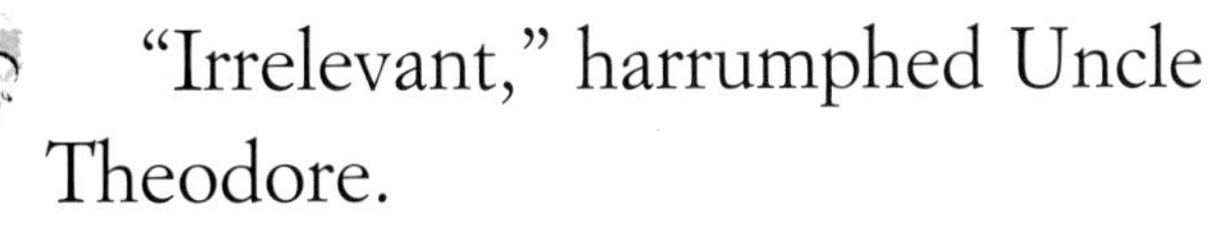

"Irrelevant," harrumphed Uncle Theodore.

"He's just a little hungry, that's all," said Alice Jayne.

"Perhaps the zoo would take him," said Father, worriedly.

"He needs a real home!" cried Alice Jayne.

"We'll think about it, dear," said Mother, and she sent them all to bed.

The Christmas Crocodile didn't mean to be bad, not really. But in the middle of the night he ate through the back room door, swallowed twenty-nine crumpets on the kitchen counter, a box of pralines, one fruitcake, five golden oranges, the left stove-top burner, and a plate of ginger star cookies—they were for Santa!

Then he crept upstairs. One door was open just a bit. He nuzzled it open a bit more. Inside, he found tasty talcum powder, a feather boa that tickled his tongue, and a swig of perfume. Just right! Then he found ten pink toes. He sniffed them. Hmmmmm. He licked them. Yummmmm. He took a teeny, tiny bite.

Aunt Figgy's scream shivered cobwebs in the attic, and made the dust dance on a bottle of wine in the cellar.

"I'll save you!" roared Uncle Theodore, waking with a start from a dream about cannibals.

"Run for your lives!" shrieked Cousin Elwood.

"There's blood!" gasped Aunt Figgy, pointing to a pinprick of red on her little toe.

"Where is he?" sighed Mother.

AAAaaahhhhhh!!!!!!!

The Christmas Crocodile didn't mean to be bad, not really. They found him hiding under Alice Jayne's bed. He tried to wag his tail in a friendly fashion, but it was too cramped.

"Into the cellar with him!" commanded Father.

The Christmas Crocodile scooted sadly down the stairs to the basement. He shivered in the cold, but Alice Jayne crossed her arms and tapped her toe. She closed and locked the door with a firm click.

She went back to bed and lay under her warm blanket. She swallowed a lump in her throat.

Somehow it didn't feel like the night before Christmas anymore.

She slipped out of bed, her blanket held close, and crept quietly down the stairs to the basement.

She wrapped the Crocodile snugly, tucking her blanket under his chin. She found an old candy cane, covered with lint, in her bathrobe pocket. She broke it in two.

"One for me and one for you," she whispered.

The Christmas Crocodile gulped happily and closed his eyes.

The cellar door creaked open.

"You know, he could be an *orphan*," hissed Aunt Figgy, slipping inside. She tucked her hot water bottle under the Crocodile's toes.

"A crocodile saved my life once," announced Uncle Theodore, coming in behind Aunt Figgy. "Decent chap, really." He spread his Zulu robe over the Crocodile's tail.

"Perhaps he's learned his lesson," said Father, peering around the door and holding up his red earmuffs.

"Is it time to open the presents yet?" yawned Cousin Elwood, stumbling in. He patted the Crocodile on the snout and fell asleep.

Mother came last. She spread a fluffy comforter across them all.
"We couldn't leave him alone," she said. "Not on Christmas Eve."
Everyone nodded.
The Christmas Crocodile let out a contented snore.
"Full at last," observed Father.
Everyone sighed.
Then they all settled down to wait . . .
. . . and watch.

The Christmas Crocodile didn't mean to be bad, not really. But somehow everyone fell asleep. Somehow the Crocodile slipped away. Somehow he ate through the basement door.

They found him the next morning in the parlor, looking alarmingly round.

Alice Jayne's blanket was gone.

Aunt Figgy's hot water bottle was gone.

Uncle Theodore's Zulu robe was gone.

Father's earmuffs were gone.

Mother's comforter was gone.

The Christmas tree was gone (a blue spruce!).

*All* the presents were gone . . .

except one.

"Pump his stomach!" yowled Elwood.

"Send for my elephant gun!" roared Uncle Theodore.

"Those were for the orphans!" shrieked Aunt Figgy about the missing presents.

"What's that?" asked Alice Jayne, pointing at the one small present remaining.

"If *he* didn't want it, it must be bad," Cousin Elwood announced.

"Quite so," agreed Uncle Theodore. Aunt Figgy nodded.

"I'll open it," said Alice Jayne, and she quickly tore off the ribbon.

"It's from Uncle Carbuncle!" cried Cousin Elwood.

"Good old Carbuncle," shouted Uncle Theodore.

"Carbuncle, at last," breathed Aunt Figgy.

"But we haven't got an Uncle Carbuncle," protested Alice Jayne.

Since she was right, no one knew what to say. But Alice Jayne knew. It meant that the Christmas Crocodile had been delivered to the wrong address.

And sure enough, the doorbell rang.

At the door were two deliverymen.

"Take him away," Father said, firmly.

The two men hoisted up the Crocodile and staggered down the snowy steps to a waiting van.

"Good-bye," said Alice Jayne, sadly.

The Christmas Crocodile snuffled. One great crocodile tear ran down his snout. But then he saw the sign on the delivery van.

CARBUNCLE
vegetarian
CAFE
and
REPTILIAN
PETTING ZOO
ALL
YOU CAN
EAT!
EAT, DRINK and BE WARY!

"I'll come visit soon," promised Alice Jayne as they loaded him into the van.

"Merry Christmas!" cried the deliverymen.

"Merry Christmas!" cried one and all.

The Christmas Crocodile didn't mean to be bad, not really. He waved his tail farewell, but, as the van rounded the corner, it did look rather like a deliveryman's cap in his jaws.

“Well,” sighed Mother, “peace at last.”
“Yes,” agreed everyone . . .
. . . except Alice Jayne, who didn’t say a word.